Botanical Companion to The British Pharmacopoeia

MAVEN BOOKS

Botanical Companion to The British Pharmacopoeia

HYMAN MARKS, L.R.C.S.I.,

First Prizeman in the Practice of Medicine and in Botany,
Ledwich School of Medicine

MAVEN BOOKS

Chennai   **Trichy**   **Tirunelveli**   **New Delhi**

An Imprint of **MJP Publishers**

ISBN 978-93-87867-70-3   **MAVEN Books**

All rights reserved   No. 44, Nallathambi Street,
Printed and bound in India   Triplicane, Chennai 600 005

MJP 824   © Publishers, 2020

Publisher :   **C. Janarthanan**

Publisher's Note

The legacy of a country is in its varied cultural heritage, historical literature, developments in the field of economy and science. The top nations in the world are competing in the field of science, economy and literature. This vast legacy has to be conserved and documented so that it can be bestowed to the future generation. The knowledge of this legacy is slowly getting perished in the present generation due to lack of documentation.

Keeping this in mind, the concern with retrospective acquiring of rare books has been accented recently by the burgeoning reprint industry. MAVEN Books is gratified to retrieve the rare collections with a view to bring back those books that were landmarks in their time.

In this effort, a series of rare books would be republished under the banner, "MAVEN Books". The books in the reprint series have been carefully selected for their contemporary usefulness as well as their historical importance within the intellectual. We reconstruct the book with slight enhancements made for better presentation, without affecting the contents of the original edition.

Most of the works selected for republishing covers a huge range of subjects, from history to anthropology. We believe this reprint edition will be a service to the numerous researchers and practitioners active in this fascinating field. We allow readers to experience the wonder of peering into a scholarly work of the highest order and seminal significance.

MAVEN Books

Dedicated

TO

DANIEL TOLER THOMAS MAUNSELL, M.B. Dub., M.R.I.A.,

Lecturer on Botany to the Ledwich School of Medicine, &c., &c.,

AS

A TRIVIAL BUT SINCERE MARK

OF

HIGH ESTIMATION OF HIS ABILITIES,

AND APPRECIATION AS A FRIEND,

BY

THE AUTHOR.

PREFACE.

This Pamphlet has been written with the object of supplying, to Students of Medicine, a ready means of acquiring that special information which, heretofore, they had much trouble and attendant loss of time in searching for through cumbrous works on the subject. Charts are the usual vehicles employed for conveying this kind of information, but the want of portability materially lessens their usefulness. A short sketch of the Classes and Sub-Classes of the Vegetable Kingdom has first been given, this is followed by a description of the characters, of the Natural Orders of the Plants of the British Pharmacopœia, and the Names of the Plants, with their Orders and Officinal Parts, arranged in a tabular form. I have considered it advisable to include the Linnæan Classes and Orders, as they are frequently asked by Examining Boards. Should the object in view be attained, and the labour of the Student lightened, the earnest wishes of the Author will have been amply fulfilled.

DUBLIN, *April,* 1873.

Classes of the Vegetable Kingdom.

EXOGENS.—Plants with distinct bark, wood, and pith; the wood increasing by yearly additions to its exterior; leaves reticulated; flowers usually in quinary or quaternary arrangement, and embryo dicolytedonous.

ENDOGENS.—Stem increasing by internal growth, and having no distinct pith or bark; leaves parallel veined; flowers glumiferous, or arranged in ternary order; embryo monocotyledonous.

ACROGENS.—Cryptogamic plants, with distinct stem, containing vascular tissue; leaves with forked venation, or veinless.

THALLOGENS.—Cellular cryptogamic plants.

SUB-CLASSES OF EXOGENS.

THALAMIFLORÆ.—Flowers usually dichlamydeous; stamens hypogynous.

CALYCIFLORÆ.—Flowers dichlamydeous; petals distinct or united; stamens perigynous or epigynous.

COROLLIFLORÆ. — Flowers dichlamydeous; petals united; stamens rising from the receptacle or corolla.

MONOCHLAMYDEÆ.—Flowers with a calyx, or achlamydeous. This sub-class has two sub-divisions—

1. ANGIOSPERMÆ.—Ovules contained in a pericarp.

2. GYMNOSPERMÆ.—Ovules not contained in a true pericarp.

THALAMIFLORÆ contains the following Natural Orders :—

Ranunculaceæ	Cruciferæ	Aurantiaceæ	Zygophyllaceæ
Magnoliaceæ	Polygalaceæ	Guttiferæ	Rutaceæ
Menispermaceæ	Krameriaceæ	Vitaceæ	Simarubaceæ
Papaveraceæ	Malvaceæ	Linaceæ	

CALYCIFLORA contains :—

Anacardiaceæ	Myrtaceæ	Caprifoliaceæ	Lobeliaceæ
Amyridaceæ	Granateæ	Cinchonaceæ	Styraceæ
Leguminosæ	Cucurbitaceæ	Valerianaceæ	
Rosaceæ	Umbelliferæ	Compositæ	

COROLLIFLORÆ contains :—

Ericaceæ	Loganiaceæ	Solanaceæ	Labiatæ
Oleaceæ	Gentianaceæ	Atropaceæ	
Asclepiadaceæ	Convolvulaceæ	Scrophulariaceæ	

MONOCHLAMYDEÆ contains ·—

Polygonaceæ	Lauraceæ	Piperaceæ	
Thymelaceæ	Aristolochiaceæ	Urticaceæ	} Angiospermous
Myristicaceæ	Euphorbiaceæ	Cupuliferæ	
	Coniferæ		} Gymnospermous

SUB-CLASSES OF ENDOGENS.

DICTYOGENS. — Plants with reticulated venation ; leaves usually disarticulating ; woody matter of rhizome disposed in circular, wedge-like form.

PETALOIDEÆ.—Flowers with a coloured perianth, or whorled scales.

GLUMALES.—Flowers composed of imbricated bracts.

DICTYOGENS includes Smilaceæ.

PETALOIDEÆ contains—

Scitamineæ,   Iridaceæ,   Liliaceæ,   Melanthaceæ.

GLUMALES contains—Gramineæ.

ACROGENS contains—Filices.

THALLOGENS contains—Lichens.

Characteristics of the Natural Orders.

THALAMIFLORAL EXOGENS.

RANUNCULACEÆ.—Herbs, rarely shrubs; leaves palmate or digitate, petioles dilated; sepals three to five; petals three to fifteen, often deformed; stamens indefinite, with adnate anthers; fruit achenes or follicles; seeds with minute embryo and horny albumen; containing—*Aconitum Napellus*, and *Podophyllum Peltatum*.

MAGNOLIACEÆ.—Trees or shrubs with coriaceous leaves and convolute stipules, which cover the buds, and are deciduous; flowers fragrant; sepals three to six; petals three or more. imbricate; stamens indefinite, with adnate anthers; carpels numerous, one-celled, on an elevated receptacle; embryo minute, in fleshy albumen; containing—*Illicium Anisatum*.

MENISPERMACEÆ.—Trailing shrubs; leaves simple, entire; flowers unisexual, often diœcious; stamens monadelphous or distinct; carpels on a gynophore, one-celled; fruit drupaceous, one-celled; embryo large, curved, in albumen; containing—*Jateorrhiza Columba*, and *Cissampelos Pareira*.

PAPAVERACEÆ.—Herbs abounding in milky juice; leaves alternate, usually divided, exstipulate; sepals two, caducous; petals three or four, crumpled in æstivation; stamens numerous, with adnate anthers; ovary with parietal placentation; fruit capsular; seeds with oily albumen; containing—*Papaver Rhœas*, and *Papaver Somniferum*.

CRUCIFERÆ.—Herbs with juice affording sulphur; leaves alternate; bracts none; flowers in corymbose racemes; sepals four; petals cruciate; stamens tertradynamous; ovary superior; fruit a silique or silicule; seeds attached to the replum, exalbuminous, with the radicle folded on the cotyledons; containing—*Sinapis Nigra, Sinapis Alba*, and *Cochlearia Armoracia*.

POLYGALACEÆ.—Herbs or shrubs; leaves simple, exstipulate; bracts three; flowers falsely papilionaceous; sepals five, irregular, the two inner ones usually petaloid; petals united, usually three, the anterior keel larger, and sometimes crested; stamens six to eight, monadelphous; anthers one-celled, ovary two-celled, each with a single pendulous ovule; seeds albuminous, with a straight embryo; containing—*Polygala Senega.*

KRAMERIACEÆ.—Distinguished from Polygalaceæ, by wanting the falsely papilionaceous flowers, having a simple one-celled ovary, and seeds without albumen; containing—*Krameria Triandra.*

MALVACEÆ.—Herbs or trees, leaves alternate, palmate, and stipulate; flowers axillary; calyx valvate; petals twisted; stamens monadelphous, with reniform anthers; ovary many-celled, or of many carpels, separable when ripe; seeds with little albumen; embryo curved, with twisted cotyledons; containing—*Gossypium.*

AURANTIACEÆ.—Trees or shrubs; leaves alternate, with oil glands, articulated to petiole; flowers fragrant; calyx short, bell-shaped; petals three to five, with the stamens inserted on a hypogynous disk; ovary free; fruit pulpy, many-celled; seeds exalbuminous; containing—*Citrus Bigaradia, C. Limonum,* and *C. Limetta,* also *Ægle Marmelos.*

GUTTIFERÆ.—Trees or shrubs, with resinous juice; leaves opposite, coriaceous, entire; flowers occasionally unisexual; sepals two to eight, unequal; petals regular; stamens numerous, often united; ovary one or many-celled; fruit dry or succulent; seeds exalbuminous; containing—*Garcinia Morella,* and *Canella Alba.*

VITACEÆ—Climbing shrubs, with tumid joints, and tendrils; leaves simple or compound; flowers small, green, racemose; calyx nearly entire; petals four to five, induplicate; stamens opposite the petals, inserted on a disk; ovary two-celled, ovules erect; fruit a uva; embryo small, in horny albumen; containing—*Vitis Vinifera.*

LINAeEÆ.—Herbs, with entire sessile exstipulate leaves; flowers regular; sepals three to five, imbricate; petals three to five, contorted; stamens united at base; ovary three to five-celled, with three to five styles; capsules globular; each cell with two seeds, divided by spurious dorsal partitions; no albumen; containing—*Linum Usitatissimum.*

ZYGOPHYLLACEÆ.—Herbs or trees; leaves opposite, stipulate, usually pinnate, not dotted; sepals four to five, convolute; petals clawed, imbricate; stamens eight to ten; ovary four to five-celled, style simple; fruit usually a capsule, opening by four to five valves; seeds usually albuminous; embryo green; containing—*Guaiacum Officinale.*

RUTAOEÆ.—Herbs or trees, with exstipulate dotted leaves, and perfect flowers; sepals four to five; petals four to five, or none; stamens definite, on the outside of a cup-shaped disk; ovary three to five-lobed; style single, sometimes divided near the base; fruit capsular, often separating when ripe; seeds one or two in each carpel. The Ruteæ have albuminous seeds; the Barosmeæ are exalbuminous; which has been considered sufficient to constitute them sub-orders; they contain—*Ruta Graveolens, Barosma Betulina, B. Crenulata, B. Serratifolia,* and *Galipea Cusparia.*

SIMARUBACEÆ.—Trees or shrubs, with bitter wood; leaves alternate, exstipulate, without dots, usually compound; sepals four to five; petals imbricate; stamens eight to ten, rising from hypogynous scales; ovary stalked, four to five-lobed; fruit, of drupes, round a receptacle, each with one pendulous exalbuminous seed; containing—*Picræna Excelsa.*

CALYCIFLORAL EXOGENS.

ANACARDIACEÆ.—Trees or shrubs, with resinous acrid juice, often blackening when dry; leaves exstipulate, alternate; flowers small, sometimes unisexual; sepals three to five, united; petals three to five, imbricate; stamens usually definite; ovary one-celled; styles three; ovule single, with a funicle from the base of the cell; fruit indehiscent; seeds exalbuminous; containing—*Pistacia Lentiscus,*

AMYRIDACEÆ.—Trees or shrubs; leaves compound, occasionally stipulate and dotted; calyx three to five cleft; petals three to five, valvate; stamens six to ten; ovary one to five-celled, surrounded by an annular disk; ovules in pairs; fruit dry and hard; exocarp splitting into valves; seeds anatropal, exalbuminous; containing—*Balsamodendron Myrrha*, and *Canarium Commune*.

LEGUMINOSÆ.—Herbs or trees with alternate, usually compound, stipulate leaves; calyx five cleft; petals papilionaceous or regular; stamens variable, distinct, or united in bundles; fruit a legume; seeds exalbuminous. This order has been sub-divided into three sub-orders—*Papilionaceæ, Cæsalpineæ,* and *Mimoseæ.*

PAPILIONACEÆ.—Petals papilionaceous, imbricate; the vexillum external. It contains—*Myroxylon Pereiræ, Myroxylon Toluifera, Sarothamnus Scoparius, Glycyrrhiza Glabra, Physostigma Venenosum, Astragalus Verus, Pterocarpus Santalinus, Pterocarpus Marsupium, Indigofera Tinctoria.*

CÆSALPINEÆ.—Petals imbricate; vexillum internal: includes—*Hæmatoxylum Campeachianum, Tamarindus Indica, Cassia Fistula, Copaifera Multijuga, Cassias* (producing Senna).-

MIMOSEÆ.—Petals valvate: contains—*Acacias* (yielding gum).

ROSACEÆ.—Herbs, trees, or shrubs; leaves usually compound and stipulate; flowers showy; calyx permanent, lined with a disk; petals five, equal; stamens definite or indefinite; ovaries solitary or several, distinct or united; styles obliquely inserted on the ovary; fruit variable; seeds exalbuminous; embryo straight, with flat cotyledons. Its sub-orders are :—*Amygdaleæ, Roseæ,* and *Pomeæ.*

AMYGDALEÆ.—Trees or shrubs, with deciduous calyx tube; fruit a drupe; stipules not united to the petiole. It comprises—*Amygdalus Communis, Prunus Domestica,* and *Prunus Laurocerasus.*

ROSEÆ.—Carpels not adhering to the calyx tube; fruit achenes or follicles; stipules united to petiole. Contains—*Brayera Anthelmintica, Rosa Canina, Rosa Centifolia,* and *Rosa Gallica.*

Pomeæ.—Carpels one to five, adhering more or less to the calyx tube, and to each other; fruit a pome; stipules not adhering to petiole. It contains *nothing officinal*.

Myrtaceæ.—Trees or shrubs; leaves usually opposite with transparent dots, and often with an intermarginal vein; calyx four or five cleft, adherent by its tube to the ovary; petals arising from the throat of the calyx, equal in number to its divisions; stamens many; anthers ovate, small; ovary many-celled; fruit dry or fleshy; seeds numerous, without albumen; containing—*Melaleuca Minor, Caryophyllus Aromaticus, Eugenia Pimenta*, and *Punica Granatum*. This latter was considered by David Don as the type of a natural order, which he called *Granateæ*, containing only the species of the genus *Punica*. *Granateæ* differs from *Myrtaceæ* by its leaves not being dotted, or having a marginal vein; the peculiar fruit; the seed being involved in pulp; and by its convoluted cotyledons.

Cucurbitaceæ.—Succulent climbing plants, with extra-axillary tendrils; leaves scabrous, palmately veined; flowers unisexual; calyx five-toothed; petals four to five, reticulated; stamens generally five, distinct or in three parcels, with sinuous anthers; ovary inferior, one celled, with three parietal placentæ; fruit a pepo; seeds flat, exalbuminous; containing—*Citrullus Colocynthis, Ecbalium Officinarum*.

Umbelliferæ.—Herbs; stems hollow and striate; leaves alternate, compound, and sheathing; flowers in compound umbels, with involucres, and often involucels; calyx obsolete, or five-toothed; petals five, with cleft or inflexed points; stamens five, epigynous; fruit a cremocarp, composed of two mericarps, separating from a forked central column, marked by longitudinal ridges; seed solitary; embryo minute, in horny albumen; containing—*Carum Carui, Pimpinella Anisum, Fœniculum Dulce, Anethum Graveolens, Coriandrum Sativum, Narthex Assafœtida, Galbanum, Dorema Ammoniacum, Conium Maculatum*.

Caprifoliaceæ—Shrubs or herbs, often twining; leaves opposite, exstipulate; flowers showy and fragrant; calyx four to five cleft, with bracts; corolla various; stamens alternate with its lobes; ovary three to five-celled; fruit indehiscing, one or more celled, crowned by the calyx lobes; albumen fleshy: contains—*Sambucus Nigra.*

CINCHONACEÆ.—Herbs, trees, or shrubs; leaves simple, opposite, with interpetiolar glandular stipules; inflorescence cymose; calyx adherent, entire or toothed; corolla regular; stamens attached to the corolla, alternate with its lobes; ovary two celled; fruit inferior, separating into two cocci, or indehiscent and dry, or succulent; embryo small, in horny albumen; containing—*Cinchona Calisaya, Cinchona Condaminea, Cinchona Succirubra, Cephaëlis Ipecacuanha,* and *Uncaria Gambir.*

VALERIANACEÆ.—Herbs; leaves opposite, exstipulate; flowers cymose; calyx superior, obsolete, or forming a pappus; corolla tubular, sometimes spurred; stamens one to five on corolla; ovary with one perfect, and two abortive cells; ovules pendulous; fruit dry; embryo without albumen: contains—*Valeriana Officinalis.*

COMPOSITÆ.—Herbs or shrubs; leaves extipulate, alternate or opposite; florets hermaphrodite, or unisexual; flowers in capitula, surrounded by involucres, and seated on receptacles, whence paleæ may arise; calyx adherent, entire or pappose; corolla regular or ligulate; stamens syngenesious; ovary inferior, one-seeded, with one style and bifid stigma; ovule erect, exalbuminous. Jussieu sub-divides Compositæ into three sub-orders—*Chicoraceæ, Cynaracephalæ,* and *Corymbiferæ.*

CHICORACEÆ.—Florets perfect and ligulate. Examples—*Taraxacum dens leonis,* and *Lactuca Virosa.*

CYNARACEPHALÆ.—Florets tubular, homogamous, or those of the ray neuter; style swollen below its branches. It contains *no officinal species.*

CORYMBIFERÆ.—Florets homogamous, and usually tubular, or those of the ray filiform, or tubular and pistilliferous, or ligulate; style not swollen. Examples—*Anthemis Nobilis, Artemisia, Arnica Montana,* and *Anacyclus Pyrethrum.*

LOBELIACEÆ.—Lactescent herbs or shrubs; leaves alternate, exstipulate; calyx five-partite, superior; corolla five cleft, irregular; stamens five, epigynous; anthers cohering; ovary inferior, one to three-celled; stigma fringed; fruit capsular; seeds numerous, albuminous; containing—*Lobelia Inflata*.

STYRACEÆ.—Trees or shrubs; leaves alternate, exstipulate, often with stellate hairs; calyx free, persistent; corolla five to ten cleft; stamens united at the base, and inserted into the bottom of corolla; ovary three to five-celled; ovules partly erect, partly pendulous; fruit succulent, often unilocular; seeds albuminous; containing—*Liquidambar Orientale, Styrax Benzoin*.

COROLLIFLORAL EXOGENS.

ERICACEÆ.—Shrubs or small trees; leaves rigid, evergreen; no stipules; calyx free, from four or five cleft; corolla hypogynous, four or five parted; stamens definite; anthers two-celled, often with bristle-like appendages, opening at the base or apex; ovary surrounded by a disk, becoming a berry or drupe, or half superior becoming capsular; many-celled and seeded; containing—*Arctostaphylos Uva Ursi*.

OLEACEÆ.—Trees, or shrubs; leaves opposite, simple, or pinnate; calyx persistent, sometimes absent; corolla four-cleft or none; stamens usually two; ovary two-celled; ovules two, pendulous; fruit fleshy or dry, often one-seeded by abortion; seed albuminous; embryo straight; containing—*Olea Europea, Fraxinus Grnus*, and *Fraxinus Rotundifolia*.

ASCLEPIADACEÆ. —Lactescent, often twining plants, with entire, usually opposite leaves, and interpetiolar ciliæ; calyx five-divided; corolla five-lobed, imbricate; stamens five, filaments connate; pollen in waxy masses, cohering in pairs, and attached to the stigma (which is common to the two styles), by five glands; fruit consisting of two follicles, with numerous comose seeds, albuminous; containing—*Hemidesmus Indicus*.

Loganiaceæ.—Shrubs, or trees, with opposite, entire, exstipulate leaves; calyx inferior, four or five-parted; corolla four, five, or ten-cleft, convolute or valvate; stamens varying in number; fruit a two-celled capsule, with loose placentas, or a berry, or succulent, with one or two nucules; seeds usually peltate, albuminous; containing—*Strychnos Nux Vomica.*

Gentianaceæ.—Herbs; leaves opposite, entire, often ribbed, no stipules; calyx permanent and inferior; corolla hypogynous, with twisted or plaited æstivation; stamens inserted on corolla; ovary one-celled, of two carpels, placed right and left of axis; styles two, at times united; capsule many-seeded, the margins of the valves inverted; embryo in the axis of fleshy albumen; containing—*Gentiana Lutea,* and *Ophelia Chirata.*

Convolvulaceæ.—Lactescent herbs and shrubs, usually twining; leaves alternate, exstipulate; flowers regular; calyx persistent, imbricate; corolla monopetalous, plaited; stamens five, alternate with corolline lobes; ovary free, two to four-celled; ovules one or two in each cell; capsules septifragal; seeds large, with mucilaginous albumen; embryo curved; containing—*Convolvulus Scammonia,* and *Exogonium Purga.*

Solanaceæ.—Herbs or shrubs; leaves alternate, sometimes collateral; flowers often from the axils, no bracts; calyx persistent, inferior; corolla usually regular, five-cleft, valvate; stamens five on the corolla; anthers opening by slits or pores; ovary two-celled; stigma simple; fruit capsular or baccate, with two or four cells; seeds many; embryo usually curved, albumen fleshy; containing—*Capsicum Fastigiatum,* and *Solanum Dulcamara.*

Atropaceæ.—Distinguished from Solanaceæ by having an imbricate corolla; stamens five, one sometimes sterile, with anthers dehiscing longitudinally. Properties, narcotico-acrid; containing—*Hyoscyamus Niger, Atropa Belladonna, Datura Stramonium,* and *Nicotiana Tabacum.*

Scrophulariaceæ.—Herbs or shrubs; leaves opposite or alternate, exstipulate; calyx tubular, four or five cleft, permanent; corolla irregular, imbricate; stamens didynamous, or two; ovary bilocular; carpels anterior and posterior; fruit two-celled, capsular or baccate; seeds albuminous; containing—*Digitalis Purpurea*.

LABIATÆ.—Herbs, with tetragonal stems, and opposite exstipulate leaves; often aromatic; flowers in axillary cymes; calyx tubular, persistent; corolla bilabiate; stamens didynamous, or two; ovary four-lobed; achenes one to four; seeds with little or no albumen; containing—*Lavandula Vera, Mentha Viridis, Mentha Piperita, Rosmarinus Officinalis*.

MONOCHLAMYDEOUS EXOGENS.

POLYGONACEÆ.—Herbs; leaves alternate; stipules ochreate; flowers occasionally unisexual; perianth often coloured; stamens definite; ovary of three carpels, forming a triangular, one-celled, one-seeded nut; embryo in mealy albumen; containing—*Rheum*.

THYMELACEÆ.—Shrubs with tenacious bark; leaves entire, alternate, exstipulate; flowers rarely unisexual; perianth coloured, deciduous, with a distinct tube, and four-cleft limb; stamens eight, inserted in the top of the tube; ovary free, with a single pendulous ovule; fruit, a berry or drupe; seed with or without albumen; embryo straight; containing—*Daphne Mezereum*, and *Daphne Laureola*.

MYRISTICACEÆ.--Tropical trees; bark with red-coloured juice; leaves exstipulate; flowers unisexual; perianth three to four cleft, valvate; stamens three to twelve, distinct or monadelphous; anthers extrorse; female with deciduous calyx; carpels one or many, each with an erect anatropal ovule; fruit succulent, two-valved; albumen runcinate; containing—*Myristica Officinalis*.

LAURACEÆ.—Tropical trees; leaves exstipulate, coriaceous and dotted; perianth four to six cleft, in two rows; stamens eight to twelve, three or four innermost being abortive; anthers two or four-celled, opening by valves; ovary superior, one-celled, with one or two pendulous ovules; fruit a berry or drupe; embryo with large cotyledons, exalbuminous; containing—*Cinnamomum Zeylanicum, Camphora Officinarum, Sassafras Officinale,* and *Nectandra Rodiæi.*

ARISTOLOCHIACEÆ.—Herbs, or climbing shrubs; wood arranged in separable wedges; flowers brown or greenish; perianth tubular, valvate; stamens six to twelve, epigynous, distinct, or adhering to the style and stigmas; ovary three to six-celled; ovules numerous; stigmas radiating; fruit a capsule or berry; seeds albuminous; embryo minute; containing—*Aristolochia Serpentaria.*

EUPHORBIACEÆ.—Herbs, shrubs, or trees, with acrid milky juice, very varied in foliage and inflorescence; leaves alternate, usually stipulate; flowers unisexual, with or without a perianth; stamens variable, distinct, or in bundles; ovary usually of three united carpels, each with one or two pendulous ovules, separating and dehiscing when ripe; seed with large embryo, in fleshy albumen; containing—*Croton Eluteria, Croton Tiglium, Ricinus Communis,* and *Rottlera Tinctoria.*

PIPERACEÆ.—Shrubs or herbs, stems jointed; woody tissue, arranged in wedges; leaves usually opposite or verticillate; flowers hermaphrodite, in spikes, each on a bract; no perianth; stamens two or more; ovary free, one-celled; fruit somewhat fleshy, indehiscent, one-seeded; embryo in a vitellus, outside the albumen, and at the apex of the seed; containing—*Piper Nigrum, Cubeba Officinalis,* and *Artanthe Elongata.*

URTICACEÆ.—Herbs, trees, and shrubs; leaves alternate, scabrous, stipulate; flowers unisexual or hermaphrodite, scattered, in catkins or heads; perianth usually divided, with the stamens inserted into it; filaments sometimes curved; ovary free, one or two-celled, each with one ovule. Its sub-orders are—*Urticeæ, Cannabineæ, Ulmaceæ, Moreæ,* and *Artocarpaceæ.*

URTICEÆ.—(Not officinal.)

CANNABINEÆ.—Scabrous plants with watery juice; filaments erect, indehiscent; seeds exalbuminous. Examples—*Cannabis Indica*, and *Humulus Lupulus*.

ULMACEÆ.—Trees and shrubs; leaves rough; juice watery; fruit a samara or drupe; embryo straight or curved. Example— *Ulmus Campestris*.

MOREÆ.—Trees or shrubs, rough-leaved; juice milky; fruit a sorosis or syconus; embryo hooked. Examples—*Morus Nigra* and *Ficus Carica*.

ARTOCARPACEÆ.—(Not officinal.)

CUPULIFERÆ.—Trees or shrubs; leaves simple, stipulate, often feather-veined; flowers monoecious, males in catkins; stamens five to twenty; fertile flowers, aggregate, or on a spike; ovary many-celled, within a capsule or involucre; fruit a glans; seed solitary, exalbuminous; containing—*Quercus Pedunculata* and *Quercus Infectoria*.

CONIFERÆ.—Plants abounding in turpentine, with glandular woody tissue; leaves usually acerose; flowers unisexual; males in catkins, monandrous or monadelphous; females in cones, sometimes solitary; ovules naked; embryo with oily albumen, and two or many verticillate cotyledons. The sub-orders are— *Abietineæ* and *Cuprissineæ*.

ABIETINEÆ.—Fertile flowers, in cones, with one or two inverted ovules at base of each scale.
Scales with a thickened apophysis; leaves two to five, in bundles—Pinns.
Scales without a thickened apophysis; leaves flat, solitary— Abies.
Scales without a thickened apophysis; leaves tetragonous, solitary—Piceæ.
Scales without a thickened apophysis; leaves fascicled—Larix.

CUPRESSINEÆ.—Ovules erect; fruit an indurated cone or galbulus. Example—*Juniperus*.

ABIETINEÆ contains—*Pinus Tæda, Pinus Palustris, Abies Excelsa, Abies Balsamea,* and *Pinus Sylvestris.*

CUPRESSINEÆ contains—*Juniperus Communis,* and *Juniperus Sabina.*

DICTYOGENOUS ENDOGENS.

SMILACEÆ.—Shrubby, climbing plants; leaves petiolate, jointed to the stem; flowers hermaphrodite or unisexual; perianth six-parted; stamens six; ovary three-celled; ovules orthotropal; fruit a berry, with few or many seeds; seed albuminous; contains—*Smilax Officinalis.*

PETALOIDEAL ENDOGENS.

SCITAMINEÆ.—Tropical herbs, with rhizomes, simple sheathing leaves, the veins diverging from a mid-rib; flowers rising from membranous spathes; perianth irregular, in three rows; calyx three-lobed; the corolla and staminodes each three-parted; stamens three, the two lateral abortive; anthers two-celled; capsule three-celled, many-seeded; embryo in a vitellus; containing—*Zingiber Officinale, Curcuma Longa, Elettaria Cardamomum.*

IRIDACEÆ.—Perrennial herbs, with bulbous, tuberous, or shortly creeping rhizomes; leaves equitant, flattened vertically; flowers with spathes; perianth superior, with six-petaloid segments; stamens three, extrorse; ovary inferior, three-celled, with many ovules; style one, with three petaloid stigmas; capsule loculicidal; seeds with hard albumen; containing—*Crocus Sativus.*

LILIACEÆ.—Perennial herbs, rarely arborescent, with creeping, bulbous, or fibrous rootstocks; flowers hermaprodite; perianth inferior, regular, and petaloid; stamens six; anthers opening inwards; ovary free, three-celled; style single, with a simple or three-lobed stigma; fruit a capsule or berry; seeds usually numerous; containing—*Aloe Vulgaris, Urginea Scilla.*

Melanthaceæ.—Herbs, with fibrous or bulbous roots; leaves sheathing; perianth tubular, or in six pieces; stamens six; anthers opening outwards; ovary three-celled, many-seeded; styles three; capsule dividing into three portions superiorly; albumen dense; containing—*Colchicum Autumnale, Asagræa Officinalis,* and *Veratrum Viride.*

GLUMACEOUS ENDOGENS

Graminaceæ.—Herbs with hollow stems and nodes; leaves alternate, narrow, sheathing, and ligulate; flowers in spikelets, arranged in terminal spikes, racemes, or panicles; inflorescence, consisting of alternately disposed bracts or glumes, the two lower usually empty, the upper one enclosing a smaller palea, within which is the minute flower, composed of two very minute scales; stamens one to three, with versatile anthers; and a one-celled, one-seeded ovary, having two feathery styles; fruit a caryopsis; embryo small, at the base of farinaceous albumen; containing— *Secale Cereale, Triticum Vulgare, Hordeum Distichon,* and *Saccharum Officinarum.*

ACROGENS.

Filices.—Leafy plants, with rhizomes, the fronds coiled up, before expanding, in a circinate form, and having a forked venation; fructification consisting of capsules or sporangia, usually arranged in clusters or sori, and covered with a thin membrane when young, termed the indusium, each containing numerous minute spores. In germinating the spores produce a green leafy prothallus, upon which special antheridia and pistillidia are developed, and from these arises the future plant; containing—*Aspidium Filix Mas.*

THALLOGENS.

LICHENES.—Aërial mycetals, chiefly nourished by the surrounding medium, and producing in the thallus, green bodies resembling chlorophylle, termed gonidia, arranged singly, in bundles, or moniliform rows ; fruit of sporidia, contained in asci, or with secondary fructification, seated on sporophores ; containing—*Cetraria Islandica*, and *Roccella*.

ARRANGEMENT OF OFFICINAL PLANTS.

	CLASS.	ORDER.	NATURAL ORDER.	OFFICINAL PART.
NITUM NAPELLUS—Aconite	Polyandria	Trigynia	Ranunculaceæ	Root, fresh leaves and flowering tops
LE MARMELOS—The Bael	Polyandria	Monogynia	Aurantiaceæ	Fruit
RAGALUS VERUS—Tragacanth	Diadelphia	Decandria	Leguminosæ	Gum
CIA (several undetermined species)	Polygamia	Mia	Leguminosæ	Gum
GDALUS COMMUNIS—The Almond	Mia	Monogynia	Rosaceæ	Seed—bitter and sweet varieties
THUM GRAVEOLENS—The Dill	Pentandria	gia	Umbelliferæ	Fruit
HEMIS NOBILIS—Chamomile	Syngenesia	Superflua	Compositæ	Flowers
CYCLUS PYRETHRUM—Pellitory	Syngenesia	Superflua	Compositæ	Root
EMISIA (undetermined sps)	Syngenesia	Superflua		Unexpanded flower buds
ICA MONTANA—Arnica	Syngenesia	Superflua	Compositæ	Dried rhizome and roots
TOSTAPHYLOS UVA URSI—Bearberry	Decandria	Monogynia	Ericaceæ	Leaves
OPA BELLADONNA—Belladonna	Pentandria	Monogyniu	Atropaceæ	Fresh leaves and branches, dried root and leaves
STOLOCHIA SERPENTARIA—Serpentary	Gynandria	Hexandria	Aristolochiaceæ	Dried rhizome
ANTHE ELONGATA—Matico	Diandria	Monogynia	Piperaceæ	Dried leaves
ES BALSAMEA—Balm of Fir	Mia	Monadelphia		Turpentine, termed Canada balsam
S EXCELSA—Spruce Fir	Monœcia	Monadelphia	Coniferæ	Resinous exudation—Burgundy pitch
E VULGARIS—Barbadoes Aloe	Hexandria	Monogynia	Liliaceæ	Inspissated juice
GRÆA OFFICINALIS—Cevadilla	Hexandria	Trigynia	Melanthaceæ	Dried fruit
DIUM FILIX MAS—Male Fern	Cryptogamia	Filices	Filices	Dried rhizome
OSMA BETULINA—Buchu	Pentandria	Monogynia	Rutaceæ	Leaves, dried
„ CRENULATA—Buchu	Pentandria	Monogynia	Rutaceæ	„
„ SERRATIFOLIA—Buchu	P ntandria	Mia	Rutaceæ	„
SAMODENDRON MYRRHA—Myrrh	Octandria	Mia	Amyridaceæ	Gum-resinous exudation

Botanical Name.	Cl.	Order.	Natural Order.	Official Part.
Brayera Anthelmintica—Kousso	Icosandria	Monogynia	Rosaceæ	Flrs and tops
Cocculus Palmatus—Calumba	Diœcia	Dodecandria	Menispermaceæ	Root, cut transversely and dried
Cissampelos Pareira—Pareira	c Ia	Ma	Menispermaceæ	Dried root
Cochlearia Armoracia—Horseradish	Tetradynamia	Siliculosa	Cruciferæ	Fresh root
Citrus Bigaradia—Bitter Orange	Ba	Icosandria	Aurantiaceæ	Dried ur part of rind of fruit
,, Limonum—The Lemon	Polyadelphia	Isosandria	alie	uter part of rind of fresh fruit
,, Limetta—The Lime	Polyadelphia	Icosandria	Aurantiaceæ	Juice of fruit, to prepare Citric Acid
Canarium Commune—Elemi	Diœcia	Pentandria	Amyridaceæ	Concrete resinous exudation
Cassia Fistula—Purging Cassia	Decandria	Monogynia	Leguminosæ	Pulp of pds
,, Lanceolata—Senna	Decandria	Monogynia	Leguminosæ	Leaflets } Alexandrian Senna
,, Obovata—Senna	Decandria	Monogynia	Leguminosæ	Leaflets
,, Elongata—Senna	Decandria	Monogynia	Leguminosæ	Leaflets—Tinnivelly S nma
Caryophyllus Aromaticus—Clove	Icosandria	Monogynia	Myrtaceæ	Dried unexpanded flower buds
Citrullus Colocynthis— ylth	Mia	Monadelphia	Cucurbitaceæ	Dried decorticated fruit, freed from seeds
Copaifera Multijuga—Copaiva	Decandria	Monogynia	Leguminosæ	Oleo-resin, from incisions in tr e
Canella Alba—Canella	Dodecandria	Monogynia	Guttiferæ	Bark
Carum Carui—Caraway	Pentandria	Digynia	Umbelliferæ	Rd fruit
Coriandrum Sativum—Coriander	Pentandria	Digynia	Umbelliferæ	Dried ripe fruit
um Maculatum—Spotted Hemlock	Pentandria	Dynia	Umbelliferæ	Fresh leaves and young branches, dried laves, and rd ripe fruit
Cinchona Calisaya—C. Flava	Pentandria	Monogynia	Cinchonaceæ	Bark
,, Condaminea—C. Pallida	Pentandria	Monogynia	Cinchonaceæ	,,
,, Succirubra—C. Rubra	Pentandria	Monogynia	Cinchonaceæ	,,
Cephaelis Ipecacuanha—Ipecacuanha	Pentandria	Monogynia	Cinch mæ	Root, dried
Convolvulus Scammonia—Scammony	Pentandria	Mia	Convolvulaceæ	Dried rd, and a gum im, obtained from the living root byincision
Capsicum Fastigiatum—Capsicum	Pentandria	Monogynia	Solanaceæ	Dried ripe fruit
Cinnamomum Zeylanicum—Cinnamon	Enneandria	Monogynia	Lauraceæ	Dried bark
Camphora Officinarum—Camphor	Enneandria	Monogynia	Lauraceæ	Concrete volatile oil
Croton Eluteria—Cascarilla	Monœcia	Monadelphia	Euphorbiaceæ	Bark

Botanical Name.	Class.	Order.	Natural Order.	Official Part.
ton Tiglium—Purging Croton	Monœcia	Monadelphia	Euphorbiaceæ	Oil expressed from the seeds
eba Officinalis—Cubeb Pepper	Diandria	Trigynia	Piperaceæ	Dried unripe fruit
nabis Sativa—Hemp	Diœcia	Pentandria	Urticaceæ	Dried flowering tops of female plants
cuma Longa—Turmeric	Monandria	Monogynia	Scitamineæ	Rhizome
cus Sativus—Saffron	Triandria	Monogynia	Iridaceæ	Dried stigma, and part of style
chicum Autumnale—Colchicum	Hexandria	Trigynia	Melanthaceæ	Corm, sliced and dried, and ripe seeds
raria Islandica—Iceland Moss	Cryptogamia	Lichenes	Lichenes	The entire lichen
ema Ammoniacum—Ammoniac	Pentandria	Digynia	Umbelliferæ	Gum-resin
ura Stramonium—Thorn Apple	Pentandria	Monogynia	Atropaceæ	Dried leaves and ripe seeds
italis Purpurea—Purple Foxglove	Didynamia	Angiospermia	Scrophularineæ	Dried leaves
hne Mezereum—Mezereon	Octandria	Monogynia	Thymelaceæ	Dried Bark
, Laureola—Spurge Laurel	Octandria	Monogynia	Thymelaceæ	,, ,,
enia Pimenta—Allspice	Icosandria	Monogynia	Myrtaceæ	Dried unripe berries
alium Officinarum—SquirtingCucumber	Monœcia	Monadelphia	Cucurbitaceæ	Fruit, very nearly ripe
gonium Purga—Jalap	Pentandria	Monogynia	Convolvulaceæ	Dried tubercles (root)
ttaria Cardamomum—Cardamom	Monandria	Monogynia	Scitamineæ	Dried capsules
us Carica—Fig	Polygamia	Diœcia	Urticaceæ	Dried fruit
niculum Dulce—Fennel	Pentandria	Digynia	Umbelliferæ	Fruit
xinus Ornus—Manna	Decandria	Monogynia	Oleaceæ	Concrete saccharine exudation from the stem
,, Rotundifolia—Manna	Decandria	Monogynia	Oleaceæ	Concrete saccharine exudation from the stem
sypium—various species—Cotton	Monadelphia	Polyandria	Malvaceæ	Hairs of the seed
cinia Morella—Gamboge	Dodecandria	Monogynia	Guttiferæ	Gum-resin
iacum Officinale—Guaiacum	Decandria	Monogynia	Zygophyllaceæ	Wood, and resin obtained from the stem by natural exudation, by incisions, or by heat
ipea Cusparia—Cusparia	Diandria	Monogynia	Rutaceæ	Bark
cyrrhiza Glabra—Liquorice	Diadelphia	Decandria	Leguminosæ	Root or underground stem, fresh and dried
banum (unascertained Plant)			Umbelliferæ	Gum-resin
tiana Lutea—Gentian	Pentandria	Digynia	Gentianaceæ	Dried root

Botanical Name.	Class.	Order.	N. Or.	Officinal Part.
MATOXYLUM CAMPEACHIANUM—Logwood	Decandria	Monogynia	Leguminosæ	The heart-wood sliced
IDESMUS INDICUS—Hemidesmus	Dœia	Hexandria	Asclepiadaceæ	Dried root
c ARIS NIGER—Henbane	Pentandria	Monogynia	Atropaceæ	Fresh leaves and branches, and dried leaves
MUS LUPULUS—Hop	Dœia	Pentandria	Urticaceæ	Dried strobiles of the female plant
DEUM DISTICHON—Pearl Barley	Triandria	Digynia	Gramineæ	The kind seds
CIUM ANISATUM—Star Anise	Dodecandria	Dodecagynia	Magnoliaceæ	O, distilled from the fruit
GOFERA (various species)	Diadelphia	Decandria	Leguminosæ	A blue pigment—Indigo
IPERUS COMMUNIS—Juniper	Dœia	Monadelphia	Coniferæ	Oil, ied from unripe fruit
„ SABINA—Savin	Diœcia	Monadelphia	dæ	Fresh and dried tops
ORRHIZA COLUMBA—Calumba	Dœia	Dodecandria	Menispermaceæ	Root, cut transversely and dried
„ MIERSII—Calumba	Dœia	Dodecandria	Menispermaceæ	Root, cut transversely and dried
MERIA TRIANDRA—Rhatany	Tetrandria	Monogynia	Krameriaceæ	Dried root
UM USITATISSIMUM—Flax	Pentandria	Pentagynia	Linaceæ	Seeds, termed linseed
TUCA VIROSA—Lettuce	Syngenesia	Æqualis	Compositæ	The flowering herb
ELIA INFLATA—Lobelia	Pentandria	Monogynia	Lobeliaceæ	The dried flowering herb
UIDAMBAR ORIENTALE—Storax	Decandria	Monogynia	Styraceæ	Balsam
ANDULA VERA—Lavender	Didynamia	Gymnospermia	Labiatæ	Oil, distilled from the flowers
ROXYLON PEREIRÆ—Quinquino Ee	Decandria	Monogynia	Leguminosæ	Balsam of Peru
„ TOLUIFERA—Tolu Tree	Decandria	Monogynia	Leguminosæ	Balsam of Tolu
ALEUCA MINOR—Cajuput Tree	Polyadelphia	Icosandria	Myrtaceæ	Oil, distilled from the leaves
THA VIRIDIS—Spearmint	J Dœia	Gymnospermia	Labiatæ	Oil, distill ed from the fresh flowering herb
PIPERITA—Peppermint	Didynamia	Gymnospermia	Labiatæ	Oil, distilled from the fresh flowering herb
ISTICA OFFICINALIS—Nutmeg	Dœia	Monadelphia	Myristicaceæ	Kernel of the seed
US NIGRA—Mulberry	Mia	Tetrandria	Urticaceæ	Juice of the ripe fruit
THEX ASSAFŒTIDA	Pentandria	Digynia	Umbelliferæ	Gum-resin obtained from the living root by incision
TIANA TABACUM—Tobacco	Pentandria	Monogynia	Atropaceæ	Dried leaves of Virginian bco
TANDRA RODLÆI—Greenheart Ee	Enneandria	Monogynia	Lauraceæ	Bark
ELIA CHIRATA—Chiretta	Pentandria	Dja	Gentianaceæ	The entire plant
A EUROPEA—The Oe Tree	Diandria	Monogynia	dæ	Oil, expressed from the ripe fruit

			Natural Order.	Officinal Part.
oPHYLLUM PELTATUM—May A[pp]le	Polyandria	Monogynia	Ranunculaceæ	P[l]ate, dried
PINELLA ANISUM—Anise	P[olyandria]	Digynia	[Umbe]llæ	Oil, ...ed from the fruit
AVER RHŒAS—Red Poppy	Polyandria	Monogynia	Papaveraceæ	Fresh petals
„ SOMNIFERUM—White Poppy	Polyandria	Monogynia	Papaveraceæ	Nearly ripe dried [ca]ps
YGALA SENEGA—Senega	Diadelphia	Octandria	Polygalaceæ	Dried root
RÆNA EXCELSA—Quassia	Decandria	[Mono]gynia	Simarubaceæ	Wood
TACIA LENTISCUS—Mastich	[Di]œcia	Pentandria	Anacardiaceæ	Resinous exudation obtained f[ro]m the stem by incision
ROCARPUS SANTALINUS—Red Sandal-Wood	Di[adelp]hia	[Decan]dria	Leguminosæ	Wood
„ MARSUPIUM—Kino	Diadelphia	Decandria	Leguminosæ	Inspissated juice obtained f[ro]m the trunk by incisions
YSOSTIGMA VENENOSUM—Calabar B[e]an	[Diadelp]hia	Decandria	Leguminosæ	Seed
US DOMESTICA—Plum	Icosandria	Monogynia	Rosaceæ	Dried ru[i]pe
„ LAUROCERASUS—Cherry Laurel	[Icosan]dria	[Mono]gynia	Rosaceæ	Fresh leaves
NICA GRANATUM—Pomegranite	Icosandria	Monogynia	Myrtaceæ	Dried ba[r]k of the root
ER NIGRUM—Black P[eppe]r	Diandria	Trigynia	Piperaceæ	[Dri]ed unripe [berr]ies
US TÆDA—Frankincense Pine	[Monade]lphia	Monadelphia	[Coniferæ]	Concrete turpentine—Frankincense
, SYLVESTRIS—Scotch Fir	[Monade]lphia	Monadelphia	Coniferæ	A [resi]nous liquid
, PALUSTRIS—Swamp Pine	[Monade]lphia	Monadelphia	Coniferæ	A [resi]nous liquid
ERCUS PEDUNCULATA—British Oak	[Monade]lphia	Polyandria	Cupuliferæ	Dried ba[r]k of the [s]mall branches a[n]d young s[te]ms
INFECTORIA—Gall Oak	Monœcia	Polyandria	[Cupuli]feræ	Excrescences [caus]ed by the punctures and [dep]osited ova of Diplolepis Gallæ tic[tor]iæ
TA GRAVEOLENS—Rue	Decandria	Monogynia	Rutaceæ	Oil distilled f[ro]m the fresh herb
3A CANINA—Dog Rose	Icosa[n]dria	[Monogyn]ia	Rosaceæ	R[i]pe fruit called Hips
CENTIFOLIA—Cabbage Rose	Icosandria	Polygynia	Rosaceæ	Fresh [petals], fully expanded
GALLICA—Red Rose	Icosandria	Polygynia	Rosaceæ	Fresh and dri[e]d unexpanded petals
AMNUS CATHARTICUS—Buckthorn	Pentandria	[Penta]gynia	Rhamnaceæ	Recently expressed juice of the ripe b[e]rries
MARINUS OFFICINALIS—Rosemary	Diandria	Monogynia	Labiatæ	Oil distilled f[ro]m the fl[o]wering tops

OFFICINAL PART.

um (undetermined species)	Enneandria	Trigynia	Polygonaceæ	Dried root deprived of the bark
nus Communis—Castor Oil ant	Mia	Monadelphia	Euphorbiaceæ	Oil expressed from the eeds
tlera Tinctoria—Kamala	Diœcia	Icosandria	Euphorbiaceæ	Powder which consists of the minute glands that ver the ops
ucus Nigra—The Elder	Pentandria	Trigynia	Caprifoliaceæ	Fresh flowers
is Nigra—Black Mustard	Tetradynamia	Siliquosa	Cruciferæ	Seeds
Alba—White Mrd	Tetradynamia	Siliquosa	Cruciferæ	Se ds
thamnus Scoparius—Broom	Diadelphia	Mia	Leguminosæ	The fish and dri d tops
rax Benzoin—Benzoin	Decandria	Monogynia	Styraceæ	Balsamic resin, procured by making inci-ens into the bark
chnos Nux Vomica—Nux Mia	Pentandria	Monogynia	Loganiaceæ	The seeds
le Cereale—Common Rye	Triandria	Digynia	Gramineæ	Sclerotium (compact mycelium or spawn) of ops ua, produced within the paleæ of the common rye—Ergot
num Dulcamara—Bitter-sweet	Pentandria	Monogynia	Solanaceæ	Dried young hbs, from plants which ve sd their leaves
afras Officinale—Sassafras	Enneandria	Monogynia	Lauraceæ	Dried r ot
ax Officinalis—Sarsaparilla	Diœcia	Hexandria	Smilaceæ	Dried rot
harum Officinarum—Sugar ne	Triandria	Digynia	Graminaceæ	Juice of the stem
ma Cacao—Cacao	Mia	Hexandria	Palmaceæ	Seeds, from wih a ete oil is obtained by expression and heat
axacum Dens Leonis—Dandelion	Syngenesia	Æqualis	Compositæ	Fresh and dried r ots
ticum Vulgare—Wheat	Triandria	Digynia	Graminaceæ	The grain
rindus Indica—Tamarind	Monadelphia	Triandria	Leguminosæ	Pulp of fruit
aria Gambir—Pale Catechu	Pentandria	Monogynia	Cinchonaceæ	Extract of the aves and oung shoots
s Campestris—Broad-leaved Elm	Pentandria	Digynia	Urticaceæ	Dried inner bark
inea Scilla—Squill	Hexandria	Monogynia	Liliaceæ	ulb sliced and dried
s Vinifera—Grape Vine	Pentandria	Monogynia	Vitaceæ	Ripe fruit
atrum Viride—Green Hell re	Polygamia	Monœcia	Melanthaceæ	Dried rhizome
iber Officinale—Ginger	Mia	Monogynia	Scitamineæ	Scraped and dried rhizome

Made in the USA
Monee, IL
07 July 2026

56552375R00021